I0456662

The Ronin and the Green Maiden

By

Travis Heermann

Bear Paw Publishing
Denver
www.bearpawpublsihing.com

Illustrator: Drew Baker

PAPERBACK EDITION

ISBN 978-1-62225-417-0

Bear Paw Publishing
Denver, Colorado, USA

www.bearpawpublishing.com

Ken'ishi pulled his coat tighter around him against the chill of winter. Clouds the color of sodden ash hung heavy in the sky, and the cold, wet wind seeped into his limbs in spite of the warmth of Thunder under him. Still a novice horseman, he wondered how long before his backside would become accustomed to the lacquered wooden saddle.

A woodcutter at the last crossroads had warned him the recent massive typhoon had caused a landslide that had obliterated the most direct road to his destination. His path now took him up a less-traveled road, into the more rugged reaches of the mountains, and added at least a day of travel time.

The weight of Silver Crane's scabbard against his thigh and the rattle of arrows in the quiver on his saddle formed a great comfort. The path before him seemed to grow wilder with every passing *ri*. Brooms of pine needles edged ever closer to the road. Undergrowth encroached upon the dirt path that wound through the mountain pass and down into the river-ribboned valley below. Cold mist hugged the mountain sides like wisps of shredded silk. Monkeys screamed in the canopy, taunting travelers with raucous gibbering. Half of the mountain lay behind and above him, and the other half lay below him as he made his way toward the river in the valley's crease.

He rounded a corner and reined up at what he saw.

A warrior stood in the middle of the road, standing as tall as the stallion, fully head and shoulders taller than Ken'ishi.

The man's palms clasped the hilt of a *nodachi* that stood to his chin, point down in the earth before him. One set of great callused knuckles flexed around the others. A dark, hooded gaze rose from the ground, fierce and glittering as it met Ken'ishi's. The rest of his face was concealed behind an emerald-green iron *menpo* with the countenance of a fox. Long hair hung unkempt over the man's meaty shoulders like a great mane. A threadbare robe of forest green was festooned with pine needles and bamboo leaves as if he had been rolling on the ground.

"Who goes there, samurai?" the man said.

"I am Ken'ishi, a ..." He had almost said *ronin*. "A vassal of Lord Otomo no Tsunetomo. In the eleventh month, I fought with the defense forces in Hakozaki and single-handedly slew over fifty barbarian invaders. I am the slayer of the demon bandit Hakamadare. Who are you?"

"Whither are you bound?"

"I am traveling to my lord's estate to begin my service."

"You are on the wrong road." A grim menace rose in the man's voice, pregnant with meaning.

"I have no choice. The storm closed the main road."

Ken'ishi frowned and placed his hand on Silver Crane's hilt. "And you have not given your name, warrior."

"My name is not important. All you need know is that this is my domain, and you shall not pass without a test."

Wind moaned across the misty mountainside, filling the silence between them.

The stallion snorted and shook his head.

Finally, Ken'ishi eased the horse backward. "A test?"

"A duel."

Ken'ishi stiffened for a moment, then narrowed his eyes, stretching out with his awareness to encompass the massive boulder of a man blocking the road. Legs thick as tree trunks, arms corded with muscle, a deep powerful chest, and a sword worn from battle. The man stood with the immobility of a stone.

Sliding to the ground, Ken'ishi clamped his left hand around Silver Crane's battered scabbard. "Very well." He saw now that his nose met the level of the man's breast bone. "If this is your wish."

"You speak as if your victory is a foregone conclusion."

"I fear no man in a duel."

"Oho!" The man's eyes smiled. "A brave warrior then!"

"Yes."

"A powerful warrior."

"Yes."

"A virtuous warrior."

"What are you playing at?" The challenge in the man's voice grated across Ken'ishi's nerves. "Do you dare to impugn my honor? I had no wish to slay you, but now—"

"Oho! A prickly warrior!"

"Enough!" Ken'ishi stepped toward him.

"Are you worthy to serve, samurai? Or will your suffering be your undoing?"

"What? You speak nonsense!"

The man laughed. "And now anger claims your composure. You are too easy to manipulate. Bah! Very well, here are my terms."

Ken'ishi stood now just out of reach of the man's greatsword. He could not deny that the man's strange manner and words had unsettled him, pricked at things deep within that he could not name. He reached for the emptiness again and squeezed Silver Crane's hilt with his right hand. The sword remained silent in his grip, quiescent, but attentive and sharp as a razor. Perhaps it was hungry for this man's blood.

The man said, "I shall give you one free cut. In the future, at a time of my choosing, I will come to you and demand a return stroke, whereupon I will cut with all my might. A river of your blood will stain my blade."

Ken'ishi considered this.

"Do you accept my terms?" the man said.

Ken'ishi drew his blade. "I do."

"Then know that after your stroke, you are bound by honor to offer me a return stroke on the day of my choosing." The man slid the massive great sword, with its blade as long as Ken'ishi was tall and as wide as his palm, into the long scabbard across his back. "You may have your stroke, samurai."

Ken'ishi settled into the emptiness between moments, wariness tickling him, expectation of some trick tingling with unease up and down his back. He listened for warnings from the *kami*, but the spirits of the wood and air and earth hung silent as well as if in rapt fascination or utter disregard of the outcome.

"What you waiting for, warrior?" the man said, his voice devoid of fear. "Take your stroke, or else I shall kill you on this road here and now."

Ken'ishi raised Silver Crane's curved, polished sheen high.

The man did not flinch.

Ken'ishi leaped forward, slashing. The man's neck and spine offered hardly any resistance. Ken'ishi passed behind the man and stopped, recognizing the perfection of his cut.

He heard the man's feet stumble. Something landed in the dirt and bobbled wetly.

He expected the sound of a body toppling like a felled tree, but it did not come. He spun just in time for a shock such as he had not experienced in more than three years. He saw the big man's body still standing, saw the man's severed head lying in the dirt, looking up at him dispassionately from a grotesque angle, saw the huge meaty hand reach down and pick up the head by the hair. The body turned to face Ken'ishi, and the hand raised the head to regard him.

"Well struck, samurai," said the head. "I will return at a time of my choosing and claim my stroke. Until then, fare well, and guard your virtue."

Ken'ishi tried to speak, but no words would come. A chill shot through him.

The towering headless shoulders turned away from him and strode away down the road, swinging the head lackadaisically, like a child with a bucket.

The man disappeared around the next bend in the road before Ken'ishi's body reclaimed the will to move. He looked down at the blood on this blade, on the road, the dripping trail that followed the man's path.

It had been real.

And the last time he had seen a headless body maintain its life had been during the horrific battle with the demon bandit Hakamadare, a battle that had only ended with the complete dismemberment of the demon's body and the roasting of the head until it was nothing but a blackened skull.

This man did not seem to be an oni.

But what was he?

* * *

Ken'ishi's wariness remained at high tension as he made his way down into the mountain valley. The silver-frothed river gushed and burbled down the rocky bed in the folds between mountains. Towering walls of pine trees loomed over him, shrouding their under-parts in cool shadow. The road followed the river but could hardly be called a road, little more than a pebbled trail encroached upon by mossy stones, grass, and wildflowers.

Much of the landscape around Hakozaki and the remains of Aoka had dimmed to the customary dull greens and browns of winter, but here the land was as lush and verdant as that of a perfect spring. The cold chill of the winter shores of Hakata Bay and the cold winds of the mountain pass were replaced by pleasant, moist warmth.

Thunder kept looking with hunger toward the lush grasses that lined the trailside.

"Steady," Ken'ishi said. "We must be wary."

"Bah!" the stallion said, tossing his head. "The man is gone, and I have not seen such tender grass since spring!"

"The Warrior's Path does not allow for indulgence."

The stallion snorted. "It might be said of warriors that few men indulge themselves more."

They rounded a bend in the river and found a woman kneeling at the water's edge filling her gourd.

The sight of the mounted samurai drew a gasp from

her and she fell back. Under her broad-brimmed straw hat, Ken'ishi caught sight of wide eyes and beautiful countenance. Her glossy black hair was drawn into a loose bun at the nape of her neck. Robes of pale silk, woven with intricate patterns, draped from her shoulders. These were not the garments of a peasant woman.

She stood up and bowed. "Good day, sir."

"Good day, lady. I apologize for startling you. I am Ken'ishi, a vassal of Lord Otomo no Tsunetomo."

"Please be good to me. I am Midori."

"Your name is 'green'? A strange name."

"Look closer, sir, and see why." She slipped off her hat, fully revealing her face, a simple movement but so steeped in poise and delicacy that it held his rapt attention.

Ken'ishi's breath caught at the sight of her. Only once before had he seen a woman so beautiful, and the splinter of his love for her still remained in his heart. Full lips, flawless cheeks, and eyes—

Her eyes were green.

Brimming with deep soulfulness, perhaps tinged with a bit of mournfulness, they regarded him as if she knew him and bore a strange cunning and wisdom that went beyond her indeterminate age.

He cleared his throat. "A lady of standing and wealth should not be traveling alone in the wilderness. Where are your guards?"

"Forgive me, but I am not a noble lady, nor am I rich. It is fortuitous, our meeting. I am traveling to Lord Tsunetomo's castle to entreat to serve his wife as a handmaiden."

"You have no husband? No protection? These mountains are full of bandits. I encountered one not two hours ago."

She looked away, an expression as blank as slate settling over her face. Her head tilted forward, and she brushed a few strands of crow-black hair behind her ear with fingers long and slim and graceful.

"I am sure that Lord Tsunetomo's wife would take a woman of your grace and beauty into service," Ken'ishi said. "On my honor, I shall escort you there safely."

Her face brightened like the sun emerging over a mountaintop. She clasped her hands over her heart and bowed.

He slid to the ground and offered her his hand that she might climb into the saddle.

For two more hours, Ken'ishi led the stallion and the lady down the path, but his alarm grew as the road became a trail, the trail became a footpath, and finally diminished altogether.

He was an experienced woodsman with a clear direction in mind, but tromping across trackless mountains with a lady was a bit more difficult than doing the tromping alone.

As they walked, he often felt her eyes on him, and the

buzzing of the *kami* at those times raised his awareness again that perhaps they were being watched. Perhaps she was not alone at all. Perhaps she was leading him into a trap. But what did he have that anyone would want?

Except for Silver Crane.

The underworld crime lord Green Tiger had gone to great effort to find and steal Silver Crane. Precisely why, Ken'ishi did not yet know, save that the sword was more powerful than he had ever imagined, capable somehow of shaping the flow of destiny in countless tiny ways.

Could she be leading him into some sort of trap to steal Silver Crane again?

"How did you come to be in this wilderness?" he asked.

"I have been traveling from Hizen and lost my way."

"I should say! You have gone many *ri* out of your way."

"Alas, I am just a woman, ignorant of the land."

"Why have you come so far alone? Have you no family in your home province?"

"I have no family there now."

Something in her tone, in her mien, raised the hairs on his neck. He had encountered too many strange things to overlook the holes in an incomplete tale. Nevertheless, he could do little else but let her keep her secrets. And he had sworn himself to protect her.

"What about you, sir? What of your family? Have you no wife to warm your bed?"

A slash of guilt cut through him, the memory of Kiosé's dead face, of Little Frog's savaged body. "There is no one."

"How long have you been in Lord Otomo's service?"

"Until the invasion, I was a *ronin*." He took a deep breath and felt the unfamiliarity of his new path as it unfolded before him. "I acquitted myself well during the battle and was offered a place to serve."

"A strong, handsome warrior like you should do well in the service of such a powerful lord."

His ears heated.

"In fact, you should easily find a wife more than willing to bear you a multitude of children."

Something in her voice made him look over his shoulder. Her brilliant green eyes, flecked with gold, were fixed upon him, with a little smirk playing across her lips.

"Are you a fox?" he said. He had asked one other beautiful girl that question. The memory of how the fox-maiden Haru had once lured him into her den would never leave him.

She laughed with real mirth. "If I were, do you think I would tell you?"

He grunted and kept walking. "Perhaps it would be a point of honor to be truthful."

"Is not the greatest honor to be true to one's nature? Would a trickster *kitsune* reveal her secrets to anyone who asked?"

He grunted again.

Her smile filled her words and smoothed over the foolishness he felt. "No, sir, I am not a fox. But you do not trust me."

"I met a fox once. It did not go well. I met a woman I thought was a fox once. That did not go well either."

"What shall I do to make you trust me?"

"Twice I have asked you about husband and family. Twice you have not answered."

She sighed, and for a while there was only the plodding of the stallion's hooves and Ken'ishi's footsteps in the thickening grass. "I have a husband. He is ... my curse. He is a cruel man, so large and powerful than none may stand against him."

"Where is he?"

"I do not know. I have not seen him in a very long time. I just know that he is out there, and that knowledge is an awful, awful thing. When he strikes me—" She bit back her words.

Ken'ishi's heart went out to her. "Are you running from him?"

"In a way."

He glanced at her again. Her cheeks were dry, and her captivating green eyes looked off into the forest toward what he could not guess.

* * *

Night fell, and the woods thickened around them. Ken'ishi had long since lost the trail, forcing them to follow the river to the southwest, where he hoped it would encounter a proper road.

He made camp a hundred paces up the slope from the river, lest they attract the attention of a hungry *kappa*. He tied the stallion to a tree and spread out his sleeping mat over the bed of soft grass.

Over a modest fire, he boiled water for rice and tea, and he conversed with her as the starry bowl of night heaved above them. The winter chill made its presence known again in the absence of sunlight, and she huddled next to him. He inched away and sat closer to the fire.

Her warmth radiated through the soft silken robes as he draped his blanket over her shoulders. The slope of her shoulders allowed her robe to part just enough for a deep view of her dainty breasts. He tore his gaze away and sensed a fresh smirk upon her lips.

"You are very kind," she said.

"I have sworn to protect you."

"Even from the cold?"

He occupied himself sucking a bit of rice from between his teeth.

She said, "Would you obey me if I ordered you to warm me?"

"You are not my lord."

"Perhaps not, but would you truly let your helpless charge spend the night freezing, when all it would take is the warmth of our bodies to make us both comfortable?"

"You are playing with me. Stop it."

"Do I threaten your warrior's resolve?" Her hand went to his thigh.

"I said, stop it. Please."

"You do not find me beautiful." Her lips turned into a pout.

He snorted and stood, turning on her. "What a foolish thing to say! Of course, you're beautiful! And I think you know it! What do you want from me?"

"I apologize. Please, come sit down. It is wrong of me to flirt with you. You are clearly an honorable man."

"And you are a married woman."

"So you fear my husband? If he were to catch us, or discover us somehow?"

"I fear no man."

"Please, come and sit. I promise to behave."

He sat beside her again, their shoulders a few fingers' breadths apart. The space between them filled with enough warmth to rival the fire.

"Yes, I have a husband," she said, "but it has been so long since I have seen him, and even longer since I truly enjoyed the touch of a man. I am sorry to make you uncomfortable."

Ken'ishi nodded his acceptance.

For a while they sat and watched the fire. He pulled out his flute and began to play the old mournful songs.

Her eyes glowed in the firelight as she listened, motionless, multitudes of soft emotions dancing on her face.

When he finished, her eyes glistened, deep and warm. "Ken'ishi, I have but one request before I leave you to your honor."

"What is it?"

"A kiss."

Part of him wanted to draw back, and part of him wanted to lunge for her, take her kiss, and the rest of her, too. The result was a motionless stalemate.

Her voice grew soft and husky. "Please do me this favor. Just one kiss. It has been so long."

After a long moment, he said, "Very well."

Then he leaned forward, took her petal-soft face, and kissed her.

Her warm, soft lips leaned into his, pressing with restrained desperation. She tasted of tea and rice, pine forest and bamboo grove, orchards and wildflowers. He pulled himself away, lest he lose control and devour her.

When their lips parted, she drew away from him, pulled her knees up to her chest, and wrapped herself tighter in his blanket. "Thank you," she whispered.

"Sleep now," he said. "Perhaps tomorrow we'll reach

our destination." With his heart hammering in his chest and his loins aching with heat, he lay back on the bed of grass, and waited for his breath to slow.

The morning dawned cold and overcast with the threat of rain. Ken'ishi awoke with Midori curled up close to him, and he found that her body must have warmed him during the night, in spite of his will to resist. The scent of her hair was a breath of song in his nostrils.

Her demeanor before they set out was one of sheepish reserve, quiet as she arranged her thick, glossy flow of hair. He could not help but notice the soft, fair slope of her neck, her delicate ear, the elegant tilt of her cheek, lips parted by a tender, pink tongue.

This was no peasant woman or low-ranked samurai's wife. She must be nothing less than an empress in disguise.

They traveled on, but the way grew thicker and thicker. The river banks were choked with brush, all but impossible to pass. A chill mist settled over the lush greenery, numbing his feet and hands to his very bones. Having grown up in the frosty north, he was accustomed to such cold, but Midori was not. She sat astride the horse, shivering, even wrapped in Ken'ishi's blanket.

Soon, the only clear path was to walk the riverbed. The rocky stretches of river had given way to smooth, pebbled sand, wider and slower than above.

Just as Ken'ishi was about to lead the horse into the water, she called to him, "Stop! It is too cold for you to walk in this icy river. Why not ride before me? We shall travel easier and you will stay dry."

He thought about this for a moment and could not help but agree. Within moments of walking in this water, his feet would be numb, which would make going even more difficult and treacherous. "Very well."

The stallion protested until Ken'ishi promised him a bagful of grain when they arrived in the next town.

Midori laughed. "I have never met anyone who can speak to animals. Are a *shugenja*? Or a holy man?"

"No, I just have a peculiar upbringing."

She leaned around him, waiting for him to elaborate. When he did not, she said playfully, "Ooh, so mysterious!"

"Then that makes two of us."

She laughed again. "I suppose so. We are two enigmas in the forest of mystery."

Soft breasts and a warm cheek snuggled up to his back, the hard ridge of the saddle seat the only barrier between their bodies, and he found his heartbeat picking up speed. He could not deny that her allure was powerful, but he had sworn to protect her. Bedding her would make that task far more difficult, even if he ignored the fact that she belonged to another.

"How did he lose his ear?" she asked, pointing to the

fresh scar where one of Thunder's ears should be.

"A barbarian sword. Fortunately the wound healed well, and he has a powerful spirit."

"What barbarians do you speak of?"

He twisted over his shoulder. "Where were you in the eleventh month? Kyushu was invaded! We almost fell! If not for the typhoon..." His throat caught at the thought of the storm.

She shrugged. "My village is very small. We get few visitors."

He frowned. How could she not know about the Mongol invasion and the loss of its fleet? "But the storm."

"There was no storm in my village."

"You said you were from Hizen."

"I said I came from Hizen."

"Bah! I cannot talk to you."

Along with Ken'ishi's mood, the sky grew heavier and heavier, turning the forest tapestry of lush green into dark shadows of itself.

They managed only a couple of hours of riding before the first drops of rain began to fall. Ken'ishi's mood soured at the prospect of being both cold and wet, but then Midori pointed into the dense wall of trees stretching up the mountainside, toward the shadows under a great camphor tree. "A house!"

The shadows suggested angles and walls that meant

human construction. Ken'ishi dismounted and led the stallion up the riverbank onto the slope, which was becoming more treacherous with each drop of rain.

The rain had not yet filtered to the forest floor. The thick carpet of leaves and pine needles muffled their footfalls as they approached what appeared to be a woodcutter's shack fallen into ruin. One corner of the thatched roof had collapsed, and the walls were worm-eaten and weathered. Nevertheless, it might serve to keep the rain off their heads.

"Halloo in the house!" he called, but there was no answer. He tied the horse to one of the roof supports, and investigated the interior. The air smelled of animal dung, rot, and dust. Dust coated everything from the bare wooden floor to the pocked wooden walls, hung in the air at the disturbance of his footsteps. There was however a central pit for a fire.

Midori followed him inside, her face glowing with wonder, as if this place were a palace and not a rank hovel. "Oh, it's lovely!" She clasped her hands to her chest.

He looked at her askance, wondering if she might be mad.

"Look! Here is a bit of ribbon, and the remains of some fine zori. Doubtless he made them for her. Any wife would have been proud to wear these on her feet. In this house, there was love."

The artifacts were covered in dust and the grime of years,

but there was evidence of a life here once, lives together.

"And look at this!" From a crevice in the wall, she withdrew the tattered remnants of a cloth and straw doll. "There was a child here!" The joy on her face shifted, twisted, eyes squeezing shut. She sank to her knees, head bowed, and there she sat, stroking the moldy straw and ragged cloth. "A child," she whispered. Droplets of tears fell into the dust before her knees.

He left her there and went searching the house and environs for firewood before the rain soaked everything. He returned with his arms full of branches and found her sweeping dust from the floor in great billowing clouds that jerked a sneeze out of him. She smiled at him as he entered, her eyes as bright and clear as if she had not just been weeping.

The susurration of the rain spread over the forest canopy, and the drops began to fall to the forest floor. The whisper of rain rose to a steady hiss in the chill dimness, but the fire formed a bastion of flickering warmth. They huddled together, warming themselves in silence. The rain sluiced into the corner of the room from the collapsed roof. Numerous other leaks dripped water onto spots, including the firepit, where the droplets struck patterns into the embers and hissed with steam.

"You have a strange way of looking at things," he said, after a long time. "When we came in here, I saw nothing but a ruined hovel, a place to keep off the rain. But you saw something completely different. As if you were looking through a mirror into another time."

"Does that bother you?"

"It reminds me of things my old teacher used to say, about how a man's entire world can be twisted by perception. How his thoughts can be locked into patterns he cannot escape from."

"Perhaps we are all a bit mad."

"Even though he taught me this, among many things, it is difficult not to forget in the rush and trial of life in this world. I saw abandoned trash. You saw evidence of love."

"Do you think me foolish?"

"Such emotions have no place in warrior's heart. He must be prepared to kill or die in any given moment. I have sworn to protect you. I would die to do it. And yet..." Thoughts of everything he had lost, even having lived only twenty summers, drove a spike of pain into his heart. His parents to assassins' blades. Nearly his humanity to the machinations of the fox-maiden, Haru. His foster parents to fear and distrust. His faithful canine friend, Akao, to a demon's fury. His heart to Kazuko. And poor Little Frog, and Kiose, whose love had blinded her to the fact his heart would always belong to another, no matter how he might wish it otherwise.

She leaned into him and rested her head on his shoulder.

He let her.

Her shivers of cold traveled into him through her cheek.

She began to hum a quiet song, a soft, sweet melody he did not recognize.

He let her.

His heart began to pound again. The lust for her rose in him like a demon. Thoughts of her supple flesh under his touch, under his loins, her strange, brilliant eyes looking up into his with equal measures of desire...

Then he glanced at her, and found her face tilted toward his, lips parted, eyes glimmering with yearning for his kiss.

He felt his face drawn toward hers, a relentless pull. Their lips brushed, and fire bloomed in his belly, shot sparks into his groin. She thrust her lips hungrily into his. He took her by the shoulders and pressed her away.

Her eyes were swirling pools, glimmering with desire and confusion. "Kiss me, just once more," she said.

And he did. With a power that brought the taste of blood into his mouth, he kissed her, devouring her, and her body melted to his, quiet sighs of burgeoning desire seeping from her.

Until he pushed her away.

He stood up, startling her.

"What is it?" she said.

"We cannot," he said, but the words caught in his throat like barbs. "Honor demands it. I am sorry."

He went outside and sat huddled under the eave against the side of the house, listening to the hidden rhythms of the rain over leaves and loam, letting the rain pass within a few finger-breadths of him, hoping the coolness of it could quench the fires already burning within.

The dimness of rain-soaked day faded seamlessly into night. Ken'ishi remained outside, wrapped in his blanket, clinging to the cold as a bulwark against the hot yearning. He sensed her small movements inside, huddled by the fire, sometimes snoring softly, sometimes weeping. His thoughts meandered between the lands of waking and dreams in a twisted morass of wishes and wants, anger and guilt. Love turned men into women, weakened resolve, distracted from the warrior's way, yet burned like a fire unquenchable, a searing ember embedded in his flesh.

The rain diminished overnight until by morning it had ceased.

He awoke to the sound of Midori within the hut and the smell of fresh-cooked rice and searing meat.

He sat up at the smell of meat and went within.

She smiled up at him, but her eyes were distant and clouded. "Don't be so sullen. I had some rabbit left in my pouch. Let us have breakfast and move on."

The rabbit tasted fresher than something she might have had in her pouch for two days, but it was fresh-roasted over the fire, and his stomach roared for it.

They ate in silence, mounted the horse in silence, and traveled in silence, for a while. That Midori did not press herself so tightly against him today came both as a relief and a disappointment. Perhaps it was the *kami* who told him that something about this woman was unreachable to him, in spite of her advances, that there was too much unknown hiding behind beautiful smiles.

Higher on the slope, up under the canopy, the underbrush thinned, and the going was easier. He felt certain they would cross a path or a road soon. They crossed into a grove of bamboo that drove out all other trees. Their path wound between the hard, segmented stalks.

The sound of quick hoof beats, interspersed with the stallion's, echoed through the grove. Two deer leaped into view, bouncing, running, dodging among the bamboo stalks, coming toward them.

Midori gasped with wonder.

The deer raced past them, ears and tails high.

Ken'ishi did not need the *kami* to warn him of danger. Deer never ran toward men unless running away from something even more dangerous.

A heartbeat later, heavier footfalls tore deep into the carpet of bamboo leaves, and a deep cavernous huffing came. The boar exploded through the underbrush in pursuit of the intruders. When its red, beady eyes caught sight of the horse and riders, it squealed in rage and veered toward them. With shocking speed, it was upon them.

The stallion reared, thrashing his hooves. Midori tumbled over the horse's rump onto the ground. Ken'ishi heard the heavy thump as Thunder's front hoof struck the boar's head. It squealed in greater rage and pain, but its skull was armor enough. Slaver-coated yellow tusks flashed as it lunged and tore into the horse's left side. The horse screamed.

Ken'ishi whipped out Silver Crane, but the boar was on the left side of the horse. His bow was tied to the saddle, its string safely coiled in a watertight box against the rain.

The horse stumbled. Ken'ishi leaped free, but landed hard on his back, almost losing his grip on Silver Crane. As the stallion went down, he snapped at the boar and tore a chunk of thick bristly hide from the beast's neck.

The screams of the animal adversaries merged into a cacophony of battle, great slabs of bristled muscle tensed and straining. The boar dove into the horse's belly, heedless of lethally thrashing hooves, and ripped.

The stallion stiffened and flopped onto his side.

Ken'ishi rolled to his feet and cried, "Here, beast! Taste my steel!"

Its feral eyes fixed upon him for a moment.

Then Midori began to recover from her fall, scrambling away.

It turned toward her and charged.

"No!" Ken'ishi roared and charged.

With incredible fleetness, Midori leaped into flight.

Its thrusting snout hooked her robes, ripping, halting her in mid-step.

Ken'ishi extended Silver Crane into a stretching lunge, piercing the boar's haunch. It squealed and spun toward him, almost jerking the sword out of his hand, its snout swathed in scraps of Midori's robe, scarlet-rimmed eyes glowing like flecks of pure hate. With a roar, it charged him. Ken'ishi had only a sliver of heartbeat to bring the point of his sword to bear. The tremendous weight impaled itself on the sword point halfway to the guard, and drove Ken'ishi skidding backwards on his feet for three full paces, before its momentum was arrested, its strength draining away with the blood bursting from its nose. For a long moment, man and boar stood eye-to-eye, motionless. The boar's shudder traveled up the blade into Ken'ishi's hands.

At the taste of blood, Silver Crane came alive, and power surged up his arms, like bellowed coals flaring with heat.

He dragged out the sword, raised it high, stepped to the side, and struck.

The boar's head tumbled loose with a fountain of gore. Its body fell to the side, legs running, tearing up the leaves as if still in pursuit.

The battle fury surged through Ken'ishi's blood, heating

it with the anvil strikes of his heart. He slung the blood from his blade.

Unbridled sobbing found its way into his ears. He ran to where Midori lay.

The lower half of her robes were savagely shredded. He expected to see her bare legs gashed to the bone by the boar's tusks, but only a smear of filthy slaver marred her fair thigh.

"Are you all right?" he said.

She flew up from the forest floor and flung her arms around him, sobbing and kissing his neck and cheek.

He returned her embrace, his heart thundering with heat. He thrust the point of Silver Crane into the moist earth, and took her in both arms.

Their lips crashed together, melding, parting, tongues darting, embracing.

Fire roared through him again, exploding gooseflesh all over his body, turning his manhood into a throbbing spear. A yearning heat burst from her, and she molded to him like steaming water.

The ragged folds of her robe parted at his tugging, and her questing hands found their way to his flesh.

There was no thought, only aching passion, as he pressed her down onto the bamboo leaves, and drove into her.

The scent of her musk mixed with the stench of blood in his nostrils.

Their bodies melted together in an exquisite rhythm

that brought them both to ecstasy within moments. She cried out, clutching him with arms and legs, shuddering, convulsing as he spent himself in her.

"Yes," she said.

The waves of pleasure subsided, and he rolled to the side, breath slowing.

She rolled onto him, and kissed him again. "Thank you," she said.

He gazed with wonder upon her exquisite beauty, touched her face.

Then she sat up, gathered her robes, and stood.

And kept standing higher.

And higher.

Shoulders thickened. Her hair burst into a great dark bush. She towered over him now.

He scrambled back, leaping to his feet, snatching his sword free of the earth.

Her arms lengthened, her back broadened.

She turned toward him. Her legs turned to pillars, her arms to hairy tree branches. The emerald-green *menpo* appeared on the warrior's face.

Ken'ishi raised his sword, naked from the waist down.

The massive warrior stood motionless, hands on hips.

"What are you?" Ken'ishi cried.

"I have returned to see you fulfill our bargain, samurai," the man said.

"What do you want?"

"Very simple. The stroke that you promised me."

Ice-water dashed through Ken'ishi.

The man drew his massive greatsword from the scabbard across his back. With thick-muscled arms, he handled it as if it weighed no more than a dagger. "Honor demands that you fulfill our bargain." His voice darkened with promise and threat.

He saw now that this man's eyes flickered with emerald-green, something he had not noticed before.

His mind swirled with questions about this bizarre turn of events, but there would be no denying this man. Ken'ishi had made a bargain; honor demanded that he fulfill it. This was never the end he had envisioned for himself. He had always fantasized about dying in battle for a lord, not here on some wilderness mountainside, at the hands of some nameless warrior. Nevertheless, ultimate death was the culmination of the Warrior's Path.

Ken'ishi nodded and sheathed his sword. "Take your stroke."

Without hesitation, the great blade swept up and slashed toward him. He imagined that he would be cleft from shoulder to waist to fall in two neatly severed pieces. But instead, he felt only a brushing whisper against his breast. His *kusode* fell open.

The warrior sheathed his blade.

Warm wetness flowed and spread down his chest, soaking the lips of the slice in his *kusode*. He tried to swallow the lump of surprise in his throat. "Thank you for my life."

"You might not be so quick to thank me in future." The warrior pointed to the wound, directly over Ken'ishi's heart. "This will be your undoing, samurai. You have failed this test."

Then the warrior began to shrink. The *menpo* on his face grew fur and whiskers, his bushy mane turned reddish-brown as he knelt to all fours, diminishing, until the stern, wise eyes that glimmered up at him were those of a fox.

A fox with not one but three black-tipped, bushy tails.

Faster than lightning, it spun and raced off, disappearing among the bamboo stalks.

Ken'ishi was left with the aching pain in his breast from the cut. It was a clean cut, but deep enough for bone to peek through.

The stallion stirred, and Ken'ishi moved to survey the damage the boar had done. Thunder said, "The beast has done for me, warrior."

Great gaping slashes split the flesh of the horse's legs and chest. A length of entrails peeked through a long, bloody gash in the horse's belly.

Ken'ishi said, "I am sorry, dear friend. You have been a brave mount. Any warrior would be proud to have you."

"And you a courageous master. We have found

vengeance together."

"Farewell," Ken'ishi said, and with a quick, almost painless slash, opened the stallion's jugular.

The front of his *kusode* was a wet mass of scarlet. Fortunately, among his meager belongings were a fish hook and some thread with which he could sew the cut. The wound would not be fatal, but he would have a scar over his heart for all time.

Author, freelance writer, award-winning screenwriter, poker player, biker, roustabout, and graduate of the Odyssey Writing Workshop, Travis Heermann has sold short stories to print magazines and anthologies such as *Alembical, Fiction River, Cemetery Dance*, and others. He is the author of the Ronin Trilogy, plus *Rogues of the Black Fury*, *The Wild Boys*, and *Death Wind*. Aside from his fiction work, he has contributed to dozens of roleplaying supplements, include the *Firefly Roleplaying Game*, *Legend of the Five Rings* and *d20 System*, plus the game content for White Wolf/CCP's *EVE Online*.

Contact Information

Web: www. travisheermann.com
Blog: www.travisheermann.com/blog/
Email: travis@travisheermann.com
Twitter: @TravisHeermann
Facebook: www.facebook.com/travis.heermann

DON'T MISS A SINGLE VOLUME OF
THE RONIN TRILOGY!

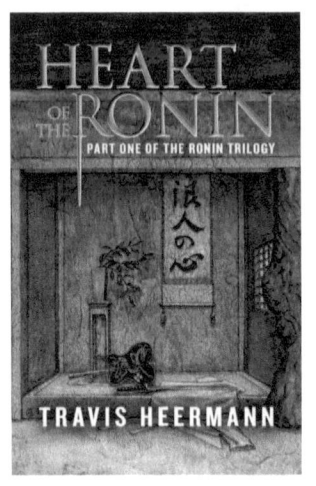

Thirteenth-century Japan is a dangerous place, even in a time of peace. Capricious gods, shape-changing animals, and bloodthirsty demons are as real and unpleasant as a gang of vicious bandits. From the wilderness emerges a young, idealistic warrior with his father's mysterious sword on his hip, a wise, sarcastic dog at his side, and a yearning in his heart to find a worthy master. He dreams only of being samurai.

Finding a master should be easy for a warrior as skilled as Ken'ishi, but the land has settled into an uneasy peace and cast multitudes of proud, powerful warriors to the four winds. These masterless warriors, ronin, often must stoop to crime and banditry to feed themselves. Ken'ishi finds himself plagued by the hatred and mistrust of peasants and samurai alike.

When he saves a noble maiden from a pack of bandits, he and his faithful dog become enmeshed in the intrigues of samurai lords, vengeful constables, Mongol spies, and a shadowy underworld crime boss known as Green Tiger. But Ken'ishi has a few secret weapons of his own, granted to him by his mysterious past and his magical upbringing. If only he knew more about his mysterious past, his parents' murder, and the sword that seems to want to talk to him....

Heart of the Ronin is an action-packed historical fantasy, set against the backdrop of ancient intrigue and impending war, the first of a sweeping three-part epic filled with deadly duels and climactic battles. Creatures of folklore and myth are as real as the katana in one's hand. And just as deadly.

"A fusion of historical fiction and adventure fantasy, the first volume of Heermann's Ronin Trilogy is a page-turning folkloric narrative of epic proportions…. [His] writing style is confident and fluid, his characters well developed and his serpentine story line anything but predictable. Numerous tantalizingly unresolved plot threads will have readers anxiously awaiting the second installment in this gripping tale of ill-fated love, betrayal and destiny." – **Publishers Weekly**

"Full of sword battles, intrigue, romance and fantastic elements blending well with historical ones, *Heart of the Ronin* is a very impressive opening in the Ronin Trilogy. It's also a page turner that you can't put down and will leave readers begging for more."– **Fantasy Book Critic**

———

In 13th-Century Japan, a land of ancient spirits, shapeshifting animals, and demons, Ken'ishi is a warrior without a master. Orphaned in infancy, he has only one link to his past—Silver Crane, his father's sword. When Silver Crane is stolen, Ken'ishi must go on a quest to recover his very identity.

The crime lord known as Green Tiger knows of Silver Crane and dreams of the day when he can destroy the shogunate and restore his shattered clan, with intrigues stretching to China, where the Mongol emperor Khubilai Khan builds an invasion fleet.

With his only weapon a wooden sword, Ken'ishi enters the shadowy world of flesh houses, Chinese smugglers, and Mongol spies.

To succeed and unleash Silver Crane's power, he must face the darkness in his own soul.

"From the first sentence, Heermann weaves a tale that sucked this reader into a rich Japanese tapestry full of ronin, samurai and magic. It was hard to put this book down to sleep." – **Patrick Hester, Hugo-Award Winning SFSignal.com and the Functional Nerds Podcast**

"*Sword of the Ronin* is a raw and energetic adventure that explores deep and eternal themes such as honor, love, and betrayal while maintaining an engaging, humorous, living world. It also has an awesome ronin hero who hacks lots of bad people to bits, if you're into that sort of thing. Which you definitely should be." – **Rich Wulf, lead writer for Legend of the Five Rings and author of The Heirs of Ash Trilogy.**

"A rich, engaging, morally complex historical fantasy, deeply embedded in Japanese culture.... *Sword of the Ronin* balances action with more intimate drama as both reader and hero question the way forward, and move through a landscape of war and legends to just the right moment of balance before the third volume. I, for one, will be looking forward to it." - **E.C. Ambrose, author of Elisha Barber, The Dark Apostle series**

———

The ronin Ken'ishi's fondest wish has been granted—he has found service with a powerful samurai lord.

But the underworld crime boss known as Green Tiger lurks in the shadows of Lord Tsunetomo's retinue, and Ken'ishi's honor is tested when learns his new master is married to Kazuko, the only woman he has ever loved. His unknown lineage holds dangerous secrets that could destroy him, and his sword, the magical relic called Silver Crane, holds the key to his past…and his future.

With enemies, temptation, and strife assailing him on all sides, Ken'ishi's very soul falls into jeopardy—even as Khubilai Khan's Mongol hordes plot their next attack.

Can Ken'ishi defeat Green Tiger, defend his homeland from the barbarian invaders, and remain true to his heart, his lord, and his honor?

If you love romance, intrigue and action on an epic scale, don't miss this stunning climax to the Ronin Trilogy!

"When you actively watch out for new writers with potential, every so often you're pleasantly surprised by one who has simply Got It, whose work is ready to push up to the next level. Travis Heermann has simply Got It." – **James A. Owen, author of** *Here, There Be Dragons*

"Lovely details, an honorable character, and great action… Travis Heermann's *Spirit of the Ronin* is a rich and entertaining story." – **Kevin J. Anderson, NYT bestselling author of** *Blood of the Cosmos, Navigators of Dune,* **and the Jedi Academy Trilogy**

www.ingramcontent.com/pod-product-compliance
Lightning Source LLC
Chambersburg PA
CBHW020321150626
46552CB00022B/3124